Karen Weaver

illustrated by Jeanette Lees

Koala

High up in the eucalyptus tree
Sits a koala as happy as can be.
Slow and sleepy,
he snoozes and eats.
Enjoying tree leaves,
his favourite treats.

Crocodile

Oh my goodness, what a smile,
You scary, scary crocodile.
You float log-like and wait for lunch,
Then snap those jaws shut
with a crunch.

Kookaburra

See the kookaburra in the tall gum tree?
He's perched on high his world to see.
His laughter rings for miles around.
It's such a happy Aussie sound.

Bilby

Mister Bilby is sure to make you smile.
He's an Easter bunny, Australian style.
In the desert where he's usually found
He burrows and tunnels
beneath the ground.

Dingo

You are as lucky as a dog can be
As you roam the country wild and free
Your hunter's howl rings clear and true
For you don't bark as most dogs do.

DOLPHIN

Little Miss Dolphin frolics and plays,
Surfing the waves in our peaceful bays.
She ducks and dives to our delight.
Oh what a friendly, welcome sight.

Echidna

The echidna has so many prickles
You wouldn't try to give him tickles.
And what a sticky tongue to eat
The ants are his special treat.

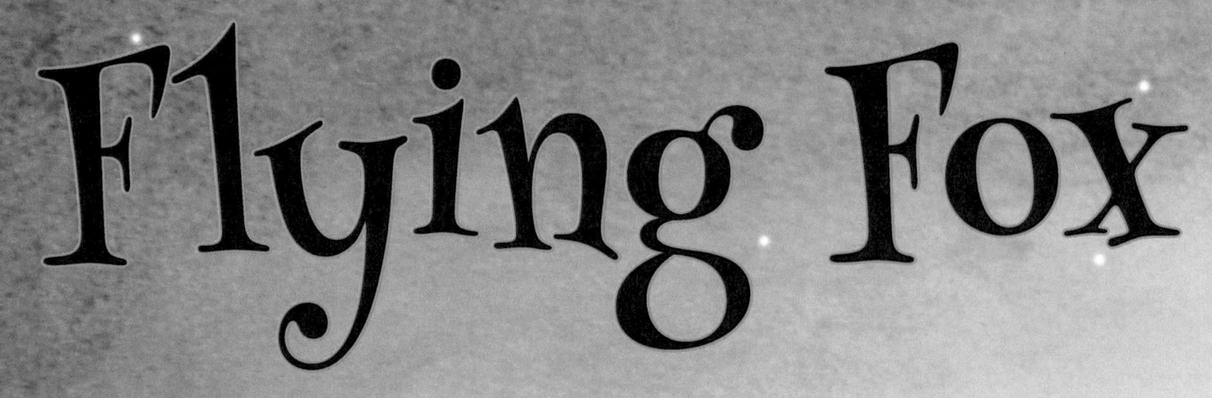

The flying fox is really a bat.
Upside down, he sleeps like that.
Using hearing and smell instead of sight
He seeks out fruit to eat at night.

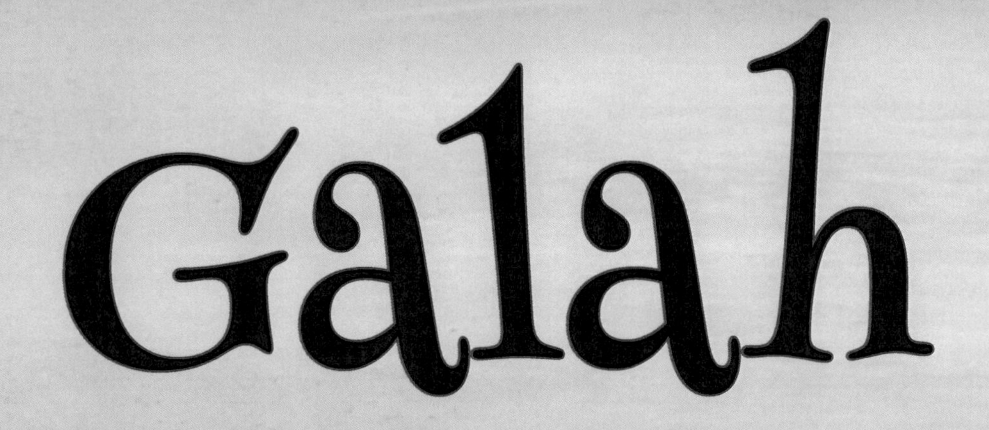

Galah

This cockatoo is so bold and loud
As it struts in pink and grey so proud.
There's trouble if the flock should feed
On the local farmer's precious seed.

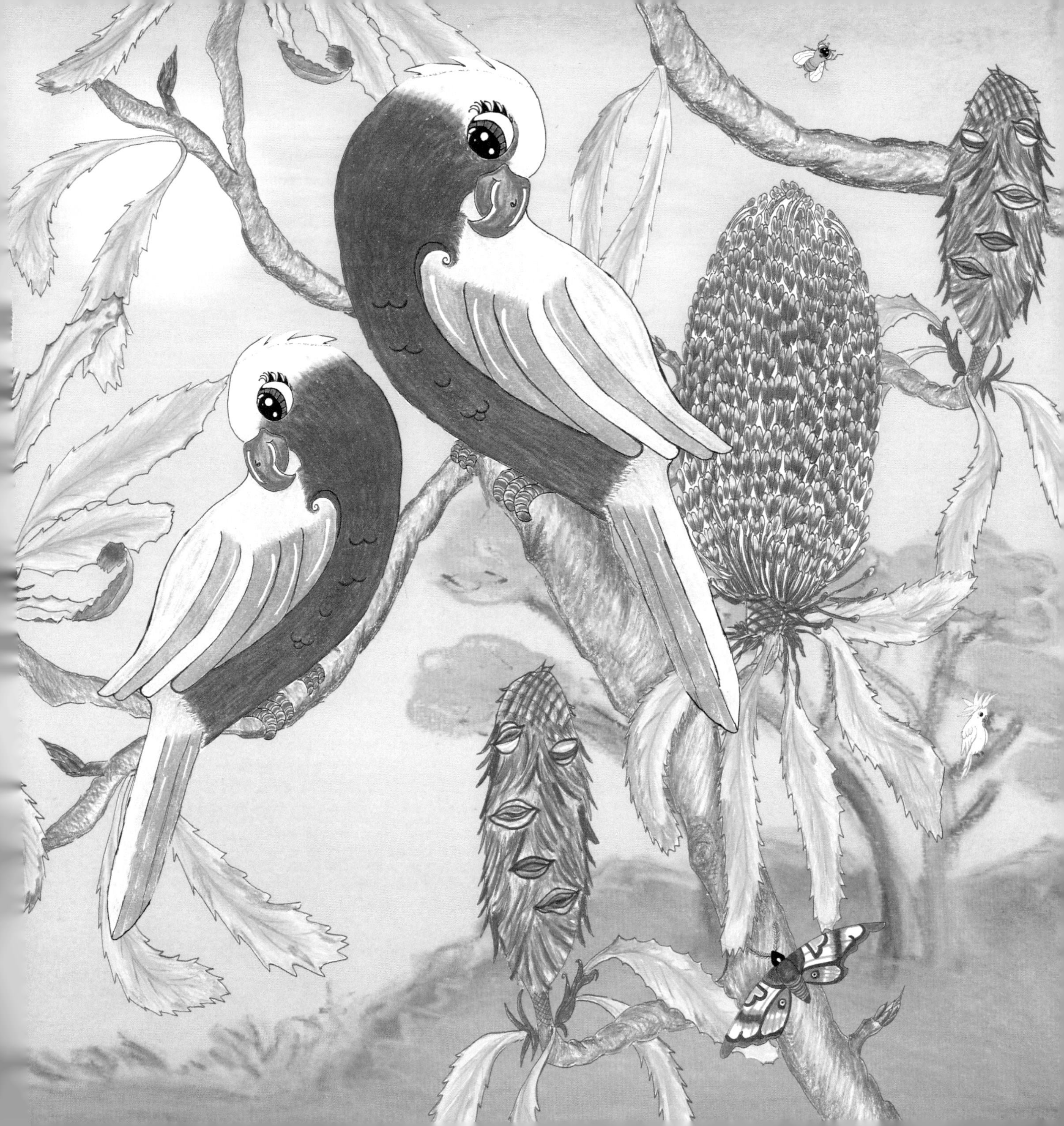

Kangaroo

G'day to you, Mrs Kangaroo.
I stopped to say, 'How do you do?'
Young Joey's snuggled in your pouch.
When you leap and bound,
does he say 'Ouch?'

Platypus

When it was introduced to folk
The platypus was thought a joke.
With beaver tail and
four webbed paws,
And a duck-like beak
instead of jaws.

Red Back Spider

The Red Back is not safe for play.
His red stripe says stay right away.
Be careful not to give him a fright.
His poison's deadly if he should bite.

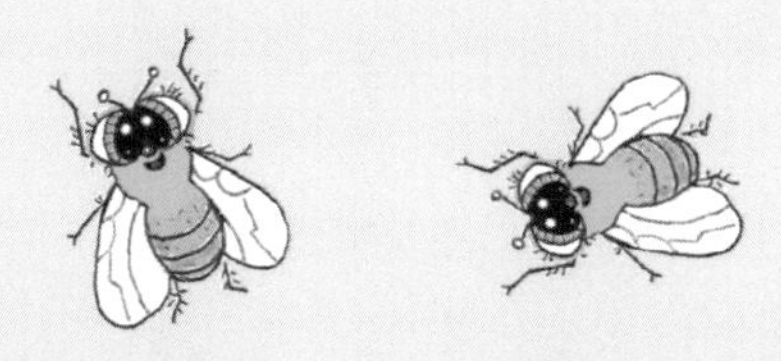

Shark

The great white shark's a fearsome beast.
You don't want to be its lunchtime feast.
Wait till it swims far away from shore
To its home in the ocean deep once more.

Emu

Mammy Emu has wings but she can't fly.
She's at home on the ground, not in the sky
She lays her eggs for Daddy Emu to hatch.
When they're born, they're hard to catch.

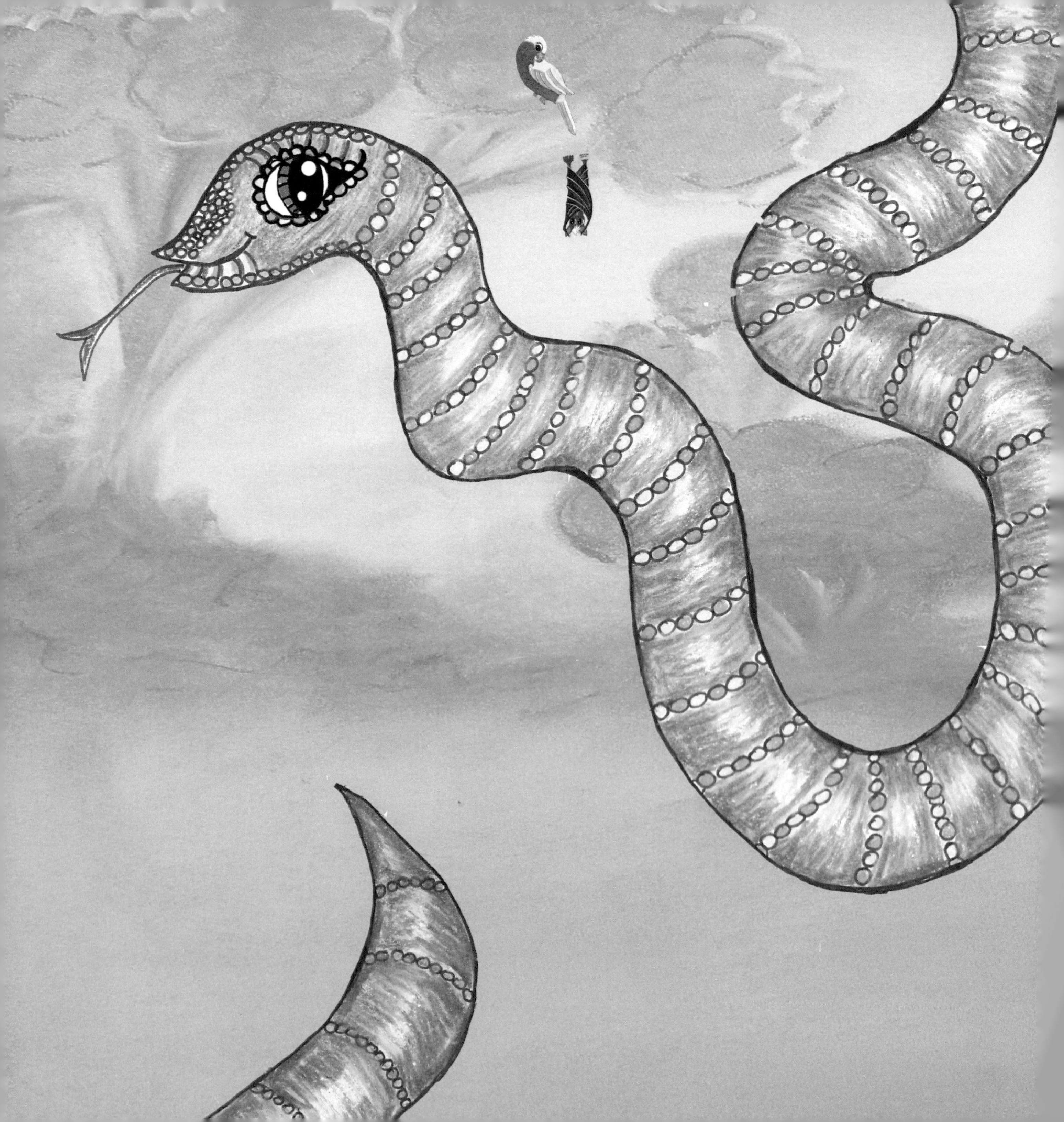

Snake

This slithery snake will strike in fear
If you should happen to go too near.
Leave it alone if you see one around
And tell an adult what you have found.

Green Tree Frog

The green tree frog is a
popular pet,
More exotic than the dogs
you've met.
He squeaks if touched and
screams at foe.
In the wild he visits homes,
you know.

Making Magic Happen Academy,
Waikiki, WA 6169

First published by Making Magic Happen Academy in 2017
www.makingmagichappenacademy.com

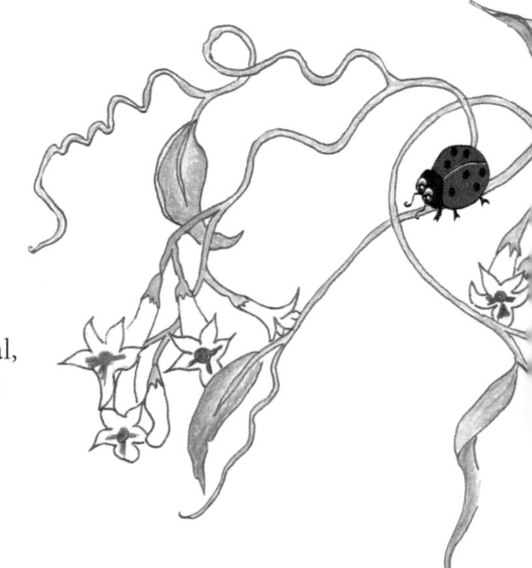

National Library of Australia
Cataloguing in-Publication entry

Karen Weaver (Karen Weaver)
Austrailian Animal Walkabout

ISBN 978-0-6480432-0-1 (sc)
ISBN 978-0-6480432-2-5 (hc)
ISBN978-0-6480432-1-8 (e)

Printed by Lightning Source AU Pty Ltd, 7 Janine Street, Scoresby, Victoria 3179, Australia
Printed by KS printing, Shangai.

Visit Karen Weaver at www.karenweaver.com
Visit Jeanette Lees at www.rosylees.com
www.makingmagichappenacademy.com

To my beautiful children
and to Australia the land we call home.
K.W

To my very special daughters
Amy and Florence.
J.L

Lightning Source UK Ltd.
Milton Keynes UK
UKRC012251051118
331834UK00002B/105